Arthur the Wizard

Written by Bryony Noble and the Growing Learners Team

Illustrated by Anastasia Vandycheva

ISBN-13: 978-1533115690
ISBN-10: 1533115699

DEDICATION AND ACKNOWLEDGMENTS

For all the children, students, teachers and parents
we have worked with.

We would like to express our gratitude for the Higher Education Innovation Funding, from the University of Portsmouth, which has enabled us to write this book.

Arthur was a wizard.

He had the tall hat.

He had the long silky robes.

He had the golden shoes.

He had everything he needed to be a wizard.

Except for one thing.

He couldn't make his spells work.

His best friend was Annie.

She made him his long, silky robes.

Arthur couldn't do spells like Annie.

Annie could do spells to make all the colours of the rainbow.

Annie could cast spells to make her fly.

Annie could cast a spell to draw beautiful pictures all over the walls, from the highest chimney, to the lowest cupboard.

She would swoop through the corridors, twisting and turning to get round a tricky corner, or over a difficult step.

Annie didn't worry about little things like tall walls or people watching her.

She covered the walls with beautiful colours, and drifted over people's heads, with colours dripping from her paint brush.

"It was not easy at the beginning!" said Annie.

"I didn't know how to match the right colours and they would often turn out all grey, dreary and dull.

Once, I even covered my assistant with sticky brown mud instead of golden glitter!

I would use my colour wheel to work out where I had gone wrong, and just try again until I got it right.

It was hard, but now I know how to make my colours shine, bright and glowing!" said Annie.

"You just need to find a strategy that works for you."

But Arthur's spells made no colours.

His spells definitely didn't make him fly.

He thought he just wasn't good enough.

"Oh dear," said Arthur, "I just don't think magic is one of my talents."

"Don't worry, Arthur," said Annie. "Every wizard can do magic."

"But nothing I do works," said Arthur.

"Well, have a look around.

Why not go and see Whizz Bang?

I'm sure he could give you some advice to help you become a better wizard!"

Arthur thought that Whizz Bang was a *very* clever wizard!

Whizz Bang could do spells to set off millions of fireworks that made a million different sounds.

Whizz Bang could cast spells to make people sing or laugh as loudly as the hugest crash of thunder, or as softly as the wind's whisper.

His spells made bangs, pops, pings, and whizzes.

The walls of Whizz Bang's lab were covered in long lists of ingredients.

Arthur could see piles of ingredients all over the table and work-tops.

There were powders and liquids and all sorts of weird and wonderful things.

Whizz Bang knew just how much of each ingredient to add to his potions, he knew how to stir them in just the right way and pour out the potion at just the right moment.

It seemed very complicated.

And it was very LOUD!

"It was not easy at the beginning!" said Whizz Bang.

"I didn't know how to get all of my potions just right, and I used to make all sorts of mess!

Once, I even made my assistant bleat like a lamb instead of sing! I just realised that I hadn't read the instructions properly.

After using the right tools and having lots of goes I finally succeeded to make my spells work," said Whizz Bang. "You just need to learn from your mistakes!"

Arthur was puzzled. He didn't think that making mistakes was something good.

He was frightened of making mistakes; he thought that it meant you were stupid.

But here was Whizz Bang saying it was okay to make mistakes because you can learn from them.

The bangs, pops, pings and whizzes made Arthur's ears hurt.

Whizz Bang seemed to like them.

He ran from bench to bench, pouring out this and shaking up that.

Arthur decided to try and make a potion like Whizz Bang.

Making the potion took a long time for Arthur. You had to get it *just* right.

Otherwise...

"Oh dear," said Arthur. "This is not one of my talents. I just can't do it!"

"Don't worry," said Annie.

"I do worry," said Arthur. "I'm not clever."

"It's not about being clever," said Annie. "It's all about practice."

"Try going to see Lily. She knows just what it takes to become a good wizard."

Arthur thought Lily was a *very* talented wizard!

Why was Lily just so good at everything?

She could cast spells to transform one single word into a super story.

Lily could cast spells so that she could speak the language of any country she visited!

Her spells made long curly lines and spindly webs of words.

She knew every book in the spell book library.

Lily always had her head in her books, she was very...quiet...

"Why is it that you know so much and can cast such amazing spells?" Arthur asked Lily.

"It was not easy at the beginning!" said Lily.

"I failed lots of times when I was trying to make my spells work. Once instead of my spell making me speak Spanish, it just gave me hiccups! You just need to practise lots!"

Arthur was confused. He didn't think that practice was something good. He believed that talents and abilities are set in stone, you either have them or you don't.

Practice, thought Arthur, means that you struggle and that you are not very clever.

Arthur continued thinking, "Hmm," he said to himself, "Lily and Whizz Bang work hard and practise and they make mistakes - I didn't realise that. I thought they were just born clever.

So perhaps it's their effort that has made them so good. It seems they didn't mind just having a go at first; they just tried their best."

Arthur wondered what he should do. He found it difficult to read all the books that Lily had read.

But... perhaps he should try again.

Arthur tried another spell.

He tried to turn a tiny fairy cake into a great big cake.

He whirled his wand, concentrated really hard and said the magic words.

BANG!

It didn't work!

The cake had got larger but then it exploded and made a mess everywhere!

He felt sad. He felt useless. He felt angry. He didn't know what else to do.

How could he make spells? He could not find them in colours.

He could not find them in potions.

He could not find them in books.

And he had been practising but he still didn't seem to be getting any better.

He went to ask Whizz Bang and Lily again.

"What do you do when you keep trying and it still doesn't work?" He asked.

"Ah," said Whizz Bang, "Ah," said Lily. "Try a different strategy!" they both said together.

"What do you mean?" said Arthur.

"Well," sighed Lily "if you keep trying to do things exactly the same way and you still can't do it then you should try a different way!"

Arthur thought whilst gazing at his hat.

He looked at the symbols on his hat.

Then he looked at the symbols on his robes. They were beautiful.

They were like the lovely colours in Annie's paintings.

They were like the weird ingredients in Whizz Bang's potions.

They were like the spiralling words in Lily's books.

But Arthur's symbols were not a painting, or a potion, or a book.
They were something else.

They could be put in patterns on a wall...they could be arranged in different piles...
they could be put in one long sentence. Each one was different.
What could these symbols mean?

Then he remembered the symbol spell book that was gathering dust in a corner of his room.

He hadn't bothered reading it until now as he thought that he was not talented enough to understand the book.

But now he remembered Lily's advice about reading a lot and practising.

He gave it a go.

He read the book and learnt about the symbols that were on his hat and on his robes.

He could recognise some, so Arthur tried something with his wand.
He gasped; when he touched the symbols he learnt about, they began to glow!
Slowly, the symbols began to move.

They wriggled. They floated off his robes and hat, and hung in the air above him.

Arthur poked them to the left, to the right, up and down, side to side.
He traced shapes with them and made pictures with them.

Arthur tried playing a game. He pretended he was making a book for Lily.
He knew a normal piece of paper was A4 size.

"So," Arthur said to himself. Let's put into practice what I've learnt. "I will put
the letter P up here; P for paper…" He found the letter hiding behind his left shoulder.
It glowed brightly, and floated into the air above him.

"I know my paper should be A4 size," Arthur muttered. "So I shall put that next to P, just
so I remember…" He found the letter A, and the number 4, and two strange swirls which
he decided to use like a hand, to hold the A and the 4.

But it didn't work. The A and the 4 would not hold together, but rather wriggled all
around the room. What was wrong?

Before he would have just given up but he remembered his friends' words of wisdom.
He remembered Whizz Bang's advice about mistakes. He gave it a go.

He went through his book and read the paragraph about how to make A4 paper and
realised that the swirls were not the right symbols to use. He corrected it with some
others.

And slowly but surely, a string of symbols was forming.

"Let's see, I think a good book should have ten pages..." Bit by bit, more and more
symbols floated off Arthur's robes into a long sentence, which was becoming his spell.

He moved his symbols around as if he were doing a jigsaw.
But he thought part of it looked a bit strange; he wasn't sure if it was working.

Then he remembered Lily's advice about different strategies. He gave it a go.

He went through his book and read about the different ways to change his symbols into
spells. Then he gently switched them round, or swapped one symbol with another. At
last, the spell seemed to be right, and the shape of a book emerged!

Just when Arthur had begun wondering what to do next...

POP!

A book appeared! A book with ten A4 pages; Arthur gasped! He touched the book's
shining cover. It was real. And slowly but surely, a string of symbols was forming.

He hurried along to Lily as fast as his feet could carry him.

"Thank you Arthur," whispered Lily. "It's beautiful."

"Would you make me the potion, the one which reproduces the song of the Bird of Paradise?" asked Whizz Bang.

Arthur wasn't sure. He didn't think it would be the same spell as last time.

But he gave it a go.

He closed his eyes and imagined what Whizz Bang would need. He collected the symbols from his robes, working it out one bit at a time.

At last...

POP!

A potion appeared!

A potion filled with silky golden liquid and colourful feathers.

Once opened, the potion delivered the crystal sound of the unique Bird of Paradise.

"Oh Arthur thank you!" cried Whizz Bang.

There was something else Arthur wanted to make.

He thought long and hard, waiting for the symbols to appear in his head, before he summoned them off his hat and robes. Eventually it took shape...

POP!

A scarf appeared!

A scarf that changes colours according to the time of the day, from midnight blue to bright sunrise yellow.

"Oh Arthur, look at what you've achieved!" said Annie, when Arthur gave her the present. "But what are you going to make for yourself?"

Arthur knew this was going to be special.

He knew it would help him make more spells. He sat and thought for a long time.

That was another problem; he didn't have a special place to sit, learn and make spells. Whizz Bang had a laboratory, Lily had a library, and Annie had the ceilings and walls.

Arthur needed his own space.

One by one, the golden symbols floated off his robes and made a shape.

It had four legs.
And four feet.
And one long body.
Finally...

POP!

Arthur had made a desk. But it was not an ordinary desk.

The four feet were curved and shiny, like the wonderful ingredients in Whizz Bang's lab. Soft swirling colours covered the desk, like the beautiful colours Annie painted with. Covering the desktop and crawling round and round the legs, were the magical symbols from Arthur's robes.

They swooped and spiralled on the desk like Lily's letters. And there was a special place for his book. Arthur sat at his new desk and felt the tingling of magic in his fingertips. This was a place all of his own, where he could learn a lot and make his own spells.

He had the tall hat.

He had the long silky robes.

He had the golden shoes.

He had a book and a desk of his own.

And he had learned to be resilient.

He had everything he needed to be a wizard.

The End.

QUESTIONS FOR DISCUSSION

What couldn't Arthur do at the beginning?

Fill in the blank: Annie said "You just need to find a _____ that works for you."

Was Arthur right to say that magic wasn't one of his talents?

Fill in the blank: Whizz Bang said "You just need to learn from your _____ ."

What did Arthur think of Whizz Bang saying that?

Was Arthur right to worry about not being clever? Why or why not?

What did Arthur think having to practise meant?

Fill in the blank: Lily said "You just need to _____ lots!"

How did Arthur feel after getting the spell with the cake wrong?

Instead of giving up, what did Arthur do?

Could Arthur cast spells after all?

What was the first thing each of the wizards said to Arthur?

What kind of mindset did Arthur have at the beginning? How did it change?

MINDSET LEARNING POINTS

Arthur thought he couldn't do spells, when really he just needed to change his strategy.

By seeking advice from many different people he learned what to do.

Because he didn't give up when something went wrong, he managed to cast a proper spell of his own.

Arthur also made some new friends as he learned!

Without changing how he approached things, he might have never learned how to cast spells.

By the end, Arthur was resilient to failures, which lead to success.

His resilience is shown by not giving up when something went wrong, but instead thinking of the advice the other wizards gave him

ABOUT THE AUTHORS

Growing Learners are a team of educational research psychologists based at the University of Portsmouth. We are passionate about supporting schools and parents to improve their children's expectations and attainment, using evidence-based practice to support them to become resilient, confident and effective learners. Everything we offer is underpinned by psychology and education theory, and applied research showing what works.

In designing materials for our intervention packages, we quickly realised that there was a need for children's story books which emphasise the Growth Mindset approach. We therefore called upon Bryony Noble, who at the time was a Creative Writing student at the university, to come and work with us.

Anastasia Vandycheva is a French professional illustrator and painter: http://www.artnastia.com/

Find out more at: http://www.port.ac.uk/department-ofpsychology/ community-collaboration/growing-learners/

Printed in Great Britain
by Amazon